The Animal Wrestlers

Joanna Troughton

CAMBRIDGE
UNIVERSITY PRESS

Long ago, in Africa, there lived a rich king. He had many beautiful things. But he was lonely.

"Go into the jungle," he said to his servant, "and choose an animal to come and live with me. Then I will have a friend."

The servant went into the jungle and
told the animals what the king wanted.

4

The animals began to quarrel because
they all wanted to live with the king. They
knew that they would be well looked after
in the palace.

The servant did not know which animal
to choose. Then he had an idea. "You must
have a wrestling match," he said. "The
winner can go and live with the king.

You will all take turns to wrestle. The winner
is the one whose back never touches
the ground."

The animals liked this idea. They began
their wrestling match.

The elephant wrestled with the hippo,

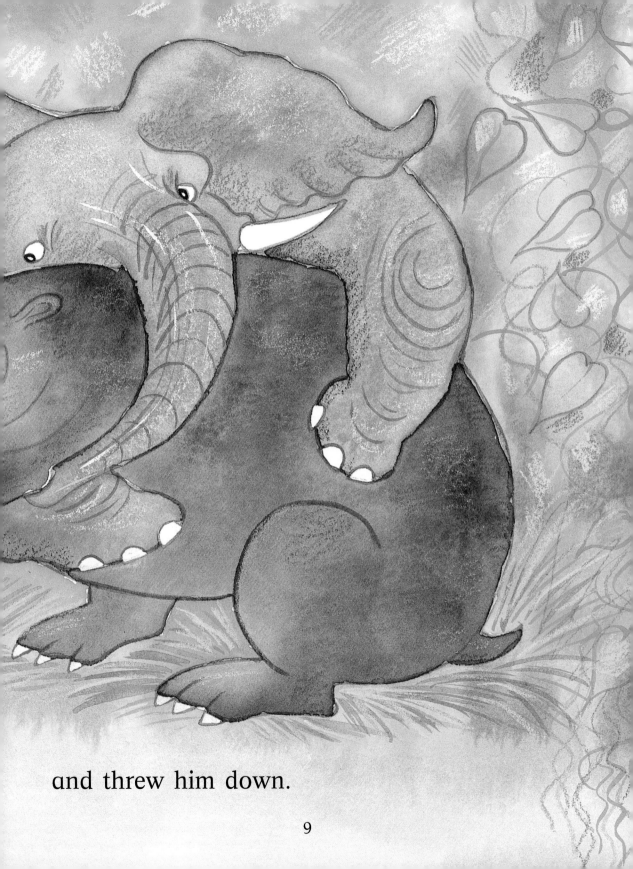

and threw him down.

The lion wrestled with the elephant,

and threw her down.

The gorilla wrestled with the lion,

and threw him down.

The crocodile wrestled with the gorilla, and threw her down.

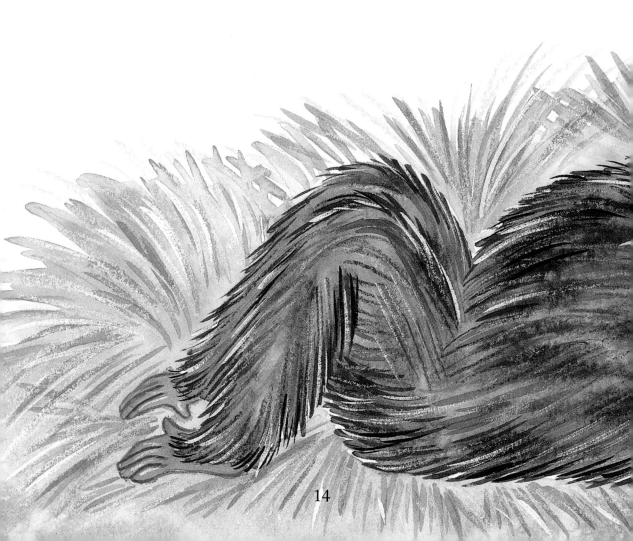

The baboon wrestled with the crocodile,
and threw him down.

The ostrich wrestled with the baboon,
and threw her down.

The zebra wrestled with the ostrich,
and threw him down.

The hyena wrestled with the zebra,
and threw her down.

Now there were only two animals left in the contest – the hyena and the cat. The cat wrestled with the hyena. But the hyena couldn't throw the cat down!

This was because the cat always landed
on her feet.

The hyena was too tired to wrestle any more.

"The wrestling match is over," said the servant. "The cat is the winner."

So the cat went to live with the king in his palace. She became the king's friend, and he looked after her very well.

From that day to this, cats have always lived with people. This is because when a cat falls down, it never lands on its back. It always lands on its feet.